Rapunzel

This book belongs to

Age_____

This edition first published in 2015 by Milly&Flynn®
an imprint of Hacche Retail Ltd
Stirling House, College Road, Cheltenham GL53 7HY
United Kingdom

www.millyandflynn.com
www.hacche.co.uk

Retold by Nina Filipek
Illustrated by Katherine Kirkland

ISBN: 978-1-909290-88-4

10 9 8 7 6 5 4 3 2

Printed and bound in China.

Rapunzel

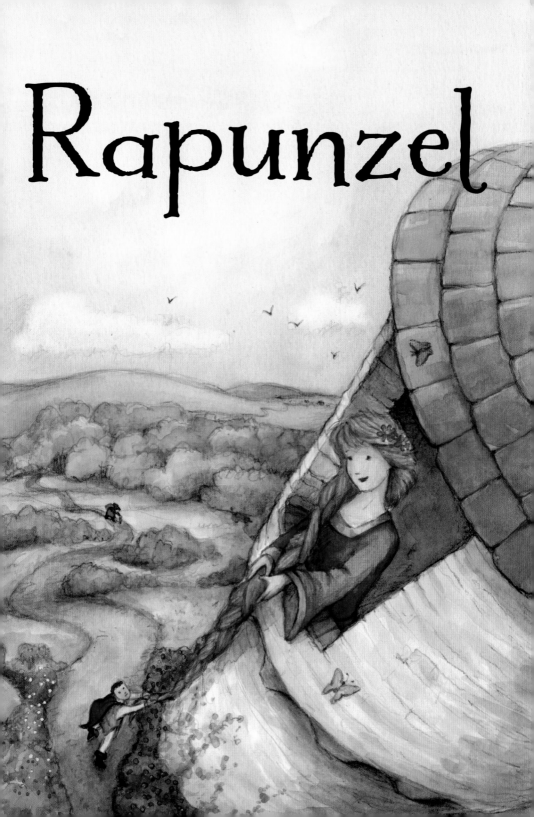

Once upon a time a husband and wife lived next door to a beautiful garden.

One day the wife longed to taste the radishes that grew there.

But there was one problem – the garden belonged to a wicked witch.

The husband thought the **wicked witch** would not notice if he took a few radishes.

7

He was very wrong! The wicked witch
caught him in her garden.
"How dare you
steal my radishes!"
she shouted.

8

The man explained how his wife longed
to taste them.

"You can take as many as you like,"

said the wicked witch,

"if you promise to give
me your first baby!"
The man was so afraid
that he agreed.

A year later, a baby girl
was born to the man and his wife.

And on that very same day the
wicked witch came and took the baby away.

The baby was called Rapunzel.

When Rapunzel grew up, the **wicked witch** locked her in a tower in the forest.

The tower had no stairs, no door and just one window at the top.

The wicked witch visited every day, calling out,

"Rapunzel!
Rapunzel!
Let down your hair!"

Rapunzel's hair had grown very long while she had been imprisoned in the tower, and the wicked witch would climb up her beautiful golden plait as if it were a rope.

One day, a handsome prince was riding in the forest when he heard Rapunzel singing.

He also heard the **wicked witch**, and saw her climb up the tower, and he was curious.

After the **wicked witch** had gone, he called out,

"Rapunzel!
Rapunzel!
Let down your hair!"

Rapunzel was very surprised to see the prince instead of the **wicked witch**!

Every day after this, the prince visited
Rapunzel in the tower.

But one day the **wicked witch** saw him.
She was furious but she waited for him to
leave. Then she climbed up the tower and
cut off Rapunzel's beautiful golden hair!

The **wicked witch** snatched
Rapunzel from the tower
and left her in a great desert.

The next day the prince called out,

"Rapunzel!
　　Rapunzel!
　　　　Let down your hair!"

So the wicked witch held Rapunzel's plait out of the window and the prince started to climb.

When the prince reached the top of the tower and saw the wicked witch, he fell back in horror!

Thorns at the bottom of the
tower blinded the prince.

"Now you
will
never
see her again!"

laughed the **wicked witch**.

For months, the prince searched for Rapunzel.

By chance, at last, he reached the great desert where she lived.

Although he could not see Rapunzel, he heard her singing.

When Rapunzel saw him she cried with
joy and her tears fell into the prince's eyes.

And then a wonderful thing happened ...

Her tears cleared the darkness away from the prince's eyes, and he was suddenly able to see again!

Together they escaped from the desert, and returned to the prince's castle, where the **wicked witch** never bothered them again.

Rapunzel and the prince got married,
and lived happily ever after.

What happens next?

Take a look at the pictures below.
Can you remember what happens next?

?

 ?

True or false?

Now that you have read the story,
can you answer these true or false
questions correctly?

1. The **wicked witch** grew carrots in her garden.
   ## True or false?

2. The **wicked witch** locked Rapunzel in a barn.
   ## True or false?

3. The prince climbed up the stairs to meet Rapunzel.
   ## True or false?

4. The **wicked witch** cut off Rapunzel's hair.
   ## True or false?

5. The prince found Rapunzel living in the desert.
   ## True or false?

Who's who?

Based on what they are saying, can you guess which character from the story each speech bubble belongs to?

Solve the puzzle ...

Here are some puzzles.
Can you solve them both?

.What is different
in this picture?

2. Help Rapunzel save her prince from
the **wicked witch** – find which
plait leads to him!